and
Finn

For the magnificent seven

First published 2007
Evans Brothers Limited
2A Portman Mansions
Chiltern St
London W1U 6NR

Reprinted 2007

British Library Cataloguing in Publication Data

Goodey, Madeline
    Fred and Finn. - (Zig zag)
    1. Frogs - Juvenile fiction 2. Children's stories
    I. Title II. Gordon, Mike
    823.9'2[J]

ISBN 978 0237 53165 2 (hb)
ISBN 978 0237 53169 0 (pb)

Printed in China

Series Editor: Nick Turpin
Design: Robert Walster
Production: Jenny Mulvanny

Fred and Finn

by Madeline Goodey

illustrated by Mike Gordon

Evans

Fat frog Finn and
thin frog Fred
were jumping up
and down.

Along came a fly.

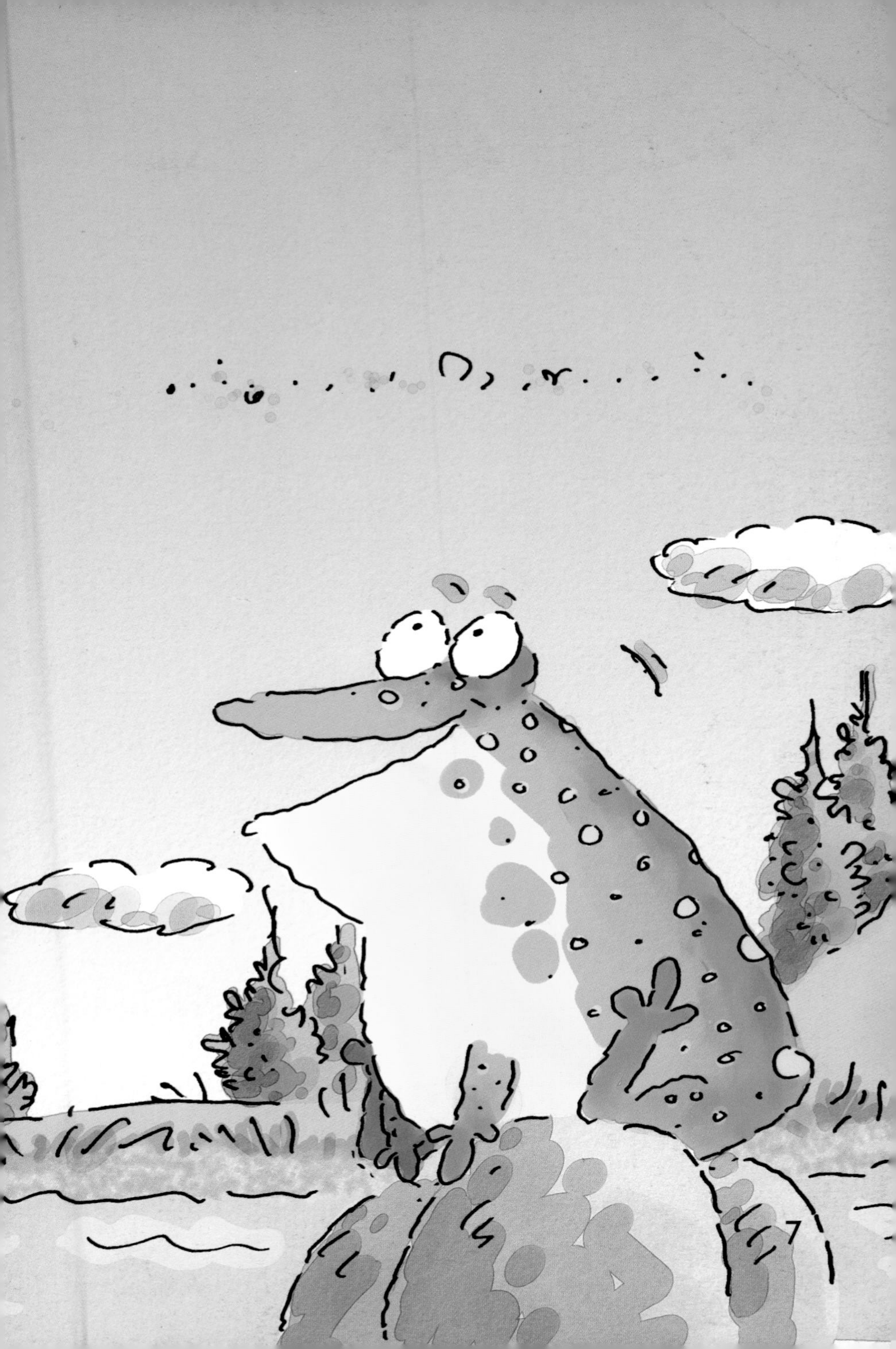

Up jumped fat Finn and grabbed that tasty fly!

Thin Fred was too slow.

Along came a slippery slug.

Down jumped fat Finn and…

...gobbled up that slippery slug.

Thin frog Fred was too slow, again.

Along came
a lovely bug.

Under the branch jumped fat frog Finn...

...and got stuck!
He couldn't move.

Thin frog Fred jumped over
the branch and ate that
lovely bug. At last!

Fat frog Finn could not move.

Thin frog Fred munched
on a juicy caterpillar.

Fat frog Finn still could
not move.

Thin frog
Fred had a
berry for his
pudding.

So fat frog Finn got thin and thin frog Fred got fat!

Why not try reading another ZigZag book?